BLACKOUTINGS

HOW I QUIT DRINKING
and Other Harrowing Tales of Alcoholism

BY TATIANA GILL

I dedicate this book
to Steve & AA, who
give me courage.

Thanks to Mark Campos and Brenda Kaslow
for helping so much with this book.

THINGS I FOUND OUT I DID
the next day (or years later) that I have no memory of

Made out with a 3-D photo of a poodle whose tongue popped in and out for an uncomfortably long time at a huge, hip party

Got it on with a coworker at a club, despite my faithful boyfriend at home.

With a crowd cheering us, made out with a coworker in front of my faithful boyfriend. Then informed him everyone at the bar hated him, including me.

Made out with a gal I was actively unattracted to while my faithful boyfriend was in the other room.

Repeatedly rolled into the fire at a SDCC* after party at the beach.
WHEEHAHA GRLBLXXSNK
*San Diego Comic Con - I owe my life to intervening cartoonists.
Insisted on walking in traffic.
crash!
I DO WHAT I WANT!
GET OUT OF THE STREET!
HEY LADY!
HONK!
screech
Had sex on someone else's front yard in a residential neighborhood
shh!
GHLXBSK
Peed on the front steps of the Performing Arts building of SCCC*
Lock your doors will you? HAH!
*Seattle Central Community College
Had sex with my manager & pulled my cable modem out of the wall - the screeching noise went on all night as I passed out & he left.
SKEE! SKREE!
SKREE!
SKREE!
Made out with a guy in the alley despite my date coming to pick me up at the bar.
BAR

Had sex with a blue-haired man on my white carpet
? ? ?
Told the EMT I had been smoking crack.
Either I was joking or somehow found crack to smoke
Went to my room to get a condom for a hookup waiting in the living room. Forgot why I was there & went to bed.
Passed out onto the floor in the middle of a concert.
ZZZ
Got it on with a guy at a party while my boyfriend was in another room.
So my boyfriend & I "opened" our relationship officially. Went on a date with that guy to a party & made out with a NEWER guy in another room.
or, so they tell me!

THINGS I WOKE UP IN

RECOVERING ALCOHOLIC COMIX BY TATIANA GILL

chocolate cake ice cream

... melted and re-hardened to my hair

(one week later)

a plate of BBQ sauce

(couldn't wash out the smell for DAYS!)

a warehouse, naked

???

I put back on my "clown suit" walk of shame in vinyl hot pants

THE HOSPITAL

IV

A compromising position with someone I'd recently told I only 'liked' them as a friend

my own bed... with a clown face imprinted on my underwear!

Every time I go for a run I cook up a new bitter, bitter, angry comic. Jogging coaxes me to cough up emotional hairballs

A LIFE WITHOUT DISTRACTION/ADDICTION = HORROR

Portrait of the Artist as an Alcoholic

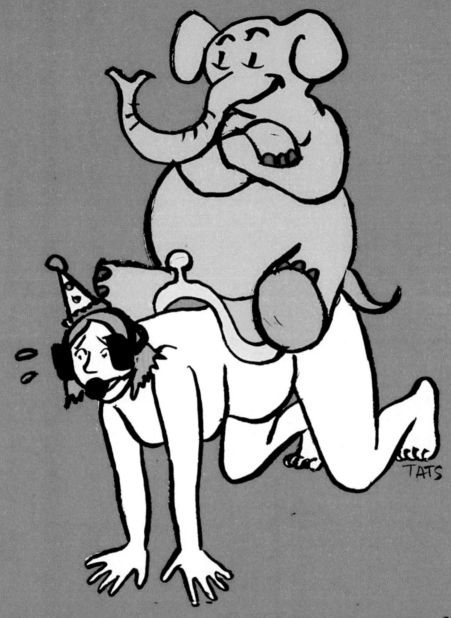

PINK ELEPHANTS

ARE

HEAVY

The other day my friend asked me, "So Tatiana, HOW DID YOU QUIT DRINKING?"

Drinking was not my problem. Life was my problem, & drinking was my cure

only it wasn't like that.

My health was jacked. I was covered in the worst eczema of my life. The doctor had run out of options, so I went to an accupuncturist

So, tell me about your habits...

WHAAAT!

She felt my organs & told me that within a few years I'd need my gall bladder removed, at the rate I was going. She begged me to drink less, & I tried, I tried...

A few months later, I went to see a new doc, more of a hippie. I asked her if she could put me on some different anxiety meds.

We never have sex!

We did last night.

really?

I'd been taking Effexor for years, which gave me more blackouts when binge drinking. I wanted a new med that mixed with booze better.

The doctor (a nurse practitioner) said to me:

OK, let's rewind that statement & listen to it again.

You don't want to black out, & your meds work. Why not...not drink?

I need to drink!

Just have one glass!

I've tried everything, I keep drinking.

Well then, quit drinking completely.

. . .

Doc: "I have one glass of wine every night when I come home, and I love it. But if I find myself looking forward to that glass by lunchtime... I skip my wine that day."

"Pot is better for you than drinking"

"quit drinking completely"

bus

"quit drinking completely"

It was January, my latest contract was ending, I was at loose ends.

I decided to quit drinking completely on January 13, 2009.

Line

I figured it would just be for a few months.

The detox was painful. My eczema exploded in infected rage.

My emotions exploded in terror & confusion.

I won't lie. I did lots of drugs to try & escape. I did ALL of the drugs, & had the worst trips of my life*

I'm too old for thiiiis!

*all those psychedelics work without booze!

Obama became president. I won't lie. I had a new lease on life!

OHGODTHANK YOUTHANKYO

I got "into" the detox. My friend Sarah sent me hand grown & mixed detox teas, I took vitamins, drank water, lemonade, & mocktails constantly

My skin being so bad kept me at home away from parties & bars

I had SO MUCH ANGER I did not know how to express. I was so mad at myself & the world. But my mouthpiece was gone.

I smoked all of the pot.

I started cleaning my room & found mold everywhere.

I started aspiring to become a Wise Woman, a teacher & healer like my coworker Kate & my acupuncturist Lesli.

I felt a new kind of relaxed, & a new hope welling inside me.

About two months in I started to notice my brain worked so much better. Reason & sanity became my new companions.

OH MY GOD I CAN FEEL IT THINKING!

EVERYTHING IS STARTING TO MAKE ...Sense!

I was still going to parties trying to hang out with drinkers, then running home in tears.

I visited old friends in CA with all the money I was suddenly saving

My allergies got better, then worse. I finally agreed to get light therapy

I read every getting-sober book I could get my hands on

I started to realize all my friends who encouraged my drinking didn't see the big picture.

I drank non alcoholic beer, Kombucha, bitters & soda, all the coffee.

I took alka seltzer cold. I felt the bitter pain of existence constantly.

I felt distant from my closest friends.

I looked around at my old friends who, instead of parties, had spent the past 2 decades building families

with their parents, their spouses, themselves, their friends. I was so, so, far behind.

All my hard work & self-dedication caught the eye of similar-minded people

I heard old friends needed help with their toddler. I volunteered to lend a hand.

That kid taught me there was joy & meaning & mystery, even sober.

This wasn't my first time not drinking. I had quit in 2005 for **3 months** (after waking up in the ER)

I'M SO BORED!

everyone is partying without me!

Well, just have a couple then!

But I'd quit pot at the same time, e was so deep in the party lifestyle - it didn't take.

During those 3 months I discovered weight melted off, I felt way better, my life was way better.

oh no he didn't!

yeesh I'm not as bad as THIS guy!

I went to a handful of AA meetings e bought a few books. I lapped up the Big Blue Book

In around 1998, my boyfriend got a DUI & was ordered to go to AA. I'd go with him sometimes to be supportive.

chugging free coffee

eating free brownies

still drinking

Boring!

assholes

hey lady, sign my slip, OK?

Despite the poor attitude, something hit home.

Tats, you should read this - it says your binge drinking is going to get worse and worse as you get older.

AA facts

HA! Good thing I refuse to think about my future!

I remembered that pamphlet. It foretold my life.

I quit drinking for one month in 2008 or so after getting dumped AGAIN. I lost a lot of weight e felt great...

OH THANK GOD!

...but as soon as the month was over, it was back on.

I did the math e my entire life, hardly one day e never a week went by without me overdoing it.

I want to DIE

my waking life was one long hangover.

I went to a couple AA meetings in 2008 with an old friend who had been passing out on the street (I only did that once!)

Is this my future?

It was downtown e packed with the homeless.

I made it my first 18 years of life only getting drunk on occasion. I was a druggie in high school but didn't drink much until college.

slumber party

Lil Tats

telling dirty jokes

Not that it was a happy 18 years. But I knew how to have a good time.

By age 19 I discovered: drinking until I puked, passed out, couldn't walk, and until I could face my own sexuality & have sex. I was regularly blacking out by 21.

Unlike most college kids I didn't "outgrow" + hot until I was 33.

Despite my drug use, my anxiety kept improving, as did my attitude & health.

"Who are you?"

I lost ALL the weight

My eczema & ensuing infection was on every inch of my body, including my scalp. 1/3 of my hair fell out.

Oh god oh god oh god

giant clumps in drain

My skin was falling off. I wrapped myself in bandages & medical tape.

My dad & stepmom asked me to see their dermatologist

I was unemployed for all of this, luckily.

I went back to my accupuncturist Lesli. I sobbed as I told her what was going on — the she lept into my lape sobbed too!

WAAH

6 ft tall 200 lbs

5 ft tall 100 lbs

WAAH

My parents doe got me to light therapy and super extra antibiotics

UVB therapy chamber

My light therapists were experts & my skin started improving

I made some unique new observations!

"Drunk people say stupid mean shit & they don't even know it!"

FUCKED UP NONSENSE

I used to think people like me were uptight bitches... now I am the bitch!

I got all "into" nutrition, gave up gluten for a few weeks, drank a daily smoothie.

My boyfriend pointed out we were no longer having our white trash scream fights.

I babysat. Just 1 year previous I never would have trusted myself with a kid.

"I live in the moment!"

"You're smarter than me, kid!"

Once my skin healed, the anger came back. I had been expressing anger by tearing my flesh with my nails

white knuckles

I tried to work through it but the teeth clenching began

More people started to tell me they knew I had a problem all along.

I wanted to drink again. My boyfriend reminded me it was better now.

Of course, he still could drink!

All the "drama" I was always caught up in disappeared.

I realized parties made me panic. I diagnosed myself with social anxiety.

I tried to "talk" myself into drinking again, but...

The evidence had arrived: I looked & felt healthier, I had a better life.

I played Fallout 3 for thousands of hours.

I got a new contract out of the blue, merchandising video games!

I was 5 months sober, my skin was better & I had a "dream job."

In my new job I realized the drinking culture in sales IS OFF THE CHAIN!

But I discovered it wasn't as hard to watch people I'd just met drink.

My stress was thru the roof. I was snappish, hysterical, crabby at home.

Of course, I was still surrounded by heavy drinkers.

I made new friendships that weren't based on enabling each other.

I had to live with the fact I was now a "square."

have a beer, buddy!

No thanks

WHY?

I don't drink

AT ALL?! Lame!!

I discovered I had no idea how to cope with the 40-hour office grind without "blowing off steam" after work.

There is not enough pot in the world to numb this anger.

I NEED A BREAK!

It occured to me (via an inspirational postcard) that by helping others I could "lose myself" in the love of a community

I had no idea how, and I was too tired to try.

I wrote that I was at the top of a giant mountain only to see a much larger mountain in front of me. So I start out & its too much, but when I look back my camp has blown away.

air too thin... too tired to go on.

What do I do?!

I discovered when I was losing my mind, I could go get a sundae instead of a drink.

things are looking up!

Maybe it was all about the blood sugar!

My hair came back! In a one-inch halo around my head.

I am a serious professional

I went to a game industry convention, & drank so much "near beer" I felt sick.

HA HA HA GOOD ONE BUDDY! I'M DRUNK TOO!

I went to see a rolfer (like a masseuse) I'd seen before I quit drinking. She was astounded at the difference in my body.

You're bouncy, loose, kinetic! Your nervous system has improved drastically!

I realized that people didn't "suck" - I just failed to treat them consistently & awesomely as an alcoholic

I'm going to take the high road?

Sobriety is like boot camp for my brain!

I was less paranoid & superstitious. I found being angry is ok (when not mixed with alcoholism!)

I found a new nervous addiction habit – cel phone games.

"I'm not ignoring the party! This IS CAREER RESEARCH!"

My new friends demanded I dump my boyfriend. This only made me dump them.

"NOBODY tells me what to do!"

"Harpies!"

My dermatologist kept my skin on the up & up

I felt like a big jerk. I'd say something & people would just stare. I stumbled over words & stopped halfway through sentences, unsure.

"and then... um... um... um..."

I was tired of being a jerk but missed my sense of self.

Old coworkers saw me & told me how much better I looked. But even non-drinkers encouraged me to drink – I looked like I needed to unwind.

"Have a cocktail! I insist!"

"No thank you..."

my boss

"What? WHY?"

My friends brought their kids & babies around. I was now child-safe

eeee

I worked in the garden. My brother & I worked on it a lot. He told me I seemed better for not drinking, when I complained about my cravings.

Between the light therapy & internal healing, I was becoming Miss Sunshine some days.

skin orange from light therapy

La La La

Compliments followed my new smile!

I started feeling loving towards lots of people

humbled empowered rested

PLEO

MAO?

KOTA

Roar!

To fill my new "empty nest" feeling I bought 2 robot dinosaurs

Instead of mulling over my unhappy childhood, I started to remember happy moments from being a kid.

I started to realize being at home alone was not so bad.

DING! WE HAVE NOW REACHED MONTH 9.

I realized my old idea "no one would like me if I didn't drink" was wrong.

I loved myself more every day.

I began to learn from my mistakes. I realized I cut myself short by being out-of-it so much.

I figured out the very pain I used alcohol to escape from was perpetuated by being drunk all the time.

I realized how much I depended on alcohol to be comfortable with my sexuality.* To find the courage to confront people with my needs

I depended on alcohol to express my fears, passions & emotions.
Thoughts from reading DRINKING: A LOVE STORY by Caroline Knapp

I wrote "The reasons we drink are our biggest obstacles when we quit. But overcoming these obstacles through hard work leads to self esteem, as opposed to the shame & regret I am used to.

I looked at some old pics I'd posted a year before.

I started 'being there' for family & old friends.

I had an art night and realized I could stay up doing art because I wouldn't be too drunk to function by 9pm.

I discovered I didn't need to mess up my life to have shame. I still had writhing episodes of shame over random, tiny mistakes.

27

I lived countless instances of things I used to do drunk, that I now did sober

FEAR
LOVE
PANIC

white knuckles ↓

I'm sober & I'm having dinner with my parents... feeling such strong emotions & floods of memories... it's almost like... TRIPPING...

Around month 10 without a drink, I had a headache.

I haven't had a headache in... TEN MONTHS! I used to have one four days a week!

My shame was getting out of control. So I came up with an action plan of doing less drugs, more drawing. Instead I immediately did a TON of drugs. It felt great until it felt awful!

3 days later

I did not quit drinking just to die from a drug related heart attack!

Some of my friends started to support me by not drinking around me. Most of my new friends didn't drink much in the first place.

Write a list of all the things you bring to your loved ones lives & why you deserve to get what you want!

I did art. I wrote. I cleaned. I worked. I treated myself to sushi. I saw friends— good ones who helped me.

I wrote "I used to get drunk to tap into any kind of outwardly expressed raw emotion" like anger or raw creative rush. Since I haven't been getting drunk, I rarely express these things. Now I'm wrasslin' with my angels

I AM A WOMAN ON THE VERGE OF EVERYTHING GOOD THINGS, BAD THINGS

IT ALL DEPENDS ON HOW I GET PUSHED & HOW I PUSH MYSELF."

I made a drawing about how my life was a shambles, a broken bloody mess, a smashed bottle I was holding onto while it cut me & I stood in my own blood.

my life's   blood

There's nothing here...nothing

I lost interest in sex & felt cut off from my sexuality

I don't want anyone to touch me —ever.

I had big panic attacks trying to deal with life —same as when I was drinking.

There's something I gotta say but I don't have the balls to say it...so I'll hold it inside until I FREAK OUT

My friend gave me great advice about speaking my mind!

I don't want to remind him every 5 minutes, I don't want to be a nag.

If you're thinking it every 5 minutes then you ARE a nag, so you may as well say it out loud!

I used to "say it out loud" by yelling it drunk!

My hair grew back as my year anniversary approached.

I got props at my job. I cried. I felt very alone. I'd lost a lot of friends & felt a wall between me & the loved ones I had.

I thought about AA, other people encouraged me to go, but I always had an excuse not to. I didn't feel safe opening up to people.

By holding my tongue because my feelings were impudent or mean, I never opened my mouth at all.

Month 11, I wrote that the brick & mortar I'd been slowly building had taken shape.

It was now a place I could come to for shelter & safety.

I enjoyed the idea of "being here now."

I like my life! I have arrived...I've arrived here, and now.

I got together with old art-and-drinking buddies & realized I remembered NOTHING about the shows we did - no names, no acts. I contributed nothing but showing up, getting drunk, & being an ass.

anything?

10 years of LIVING

anything at all?

I found an old picture of me at age 22... passed out in the middle of a party.

Oh lord.

10 years of...that.

I felt crazy. I told people to quit judging me, and they'd say they were doing nothing of the sort.

But I don't FEEL crazy! I FEEL right!

I wondered if I was picking up on things people didn't want to admit.

I learned if I took a xanax before a party, it went easier for me.

That wine looks delicious

Tats! How are you?

white knuckles

Why couldn't I have a glass? She has one. She's happy.

FROM DREW BARRYMORE AGE 13

"There is no happy ending because there is no end to the struggle for a clean & sober life. The happiness comes from knowing that you're alive and have a chance to enjoy it."

I got the bill from light therapy.

SHIT!

Very, very tan

orange actually

After insurance I was now $2000 in debt. If I skipped sessions, my eczema came back.

I had a ton of medical needs & I was too overwhelmed & scared. I flipped out on my doctor repeatedly.

We have to do a biopsy, it can be lethal!

BULLSHIT! Do you know how much this is going to COST?!

I couldn't stop worrying. I felt nauseous & didn't eat. I went to the Country Doctor. They took care of almost everything more cheaply & adjusted my meds (put my effexor dose up a little & put me on buspar.)

ah

I feel better.

I reconnected with more old friends. I went to Santarchy sober & took pictures & joined in some fun.

tossing a stuffed elf

I'd only done Santarchy wasted until that day

I had a work lunch with coworkers & came home writhing in shame—no reason.

One particularly awful day I wound up screaming into my pillow & drinking ½ bottle of robotussin SCREAMING BABY ON BUS GRIDLOCK VISIT FROM MOM

AAAAAA AAAAA

My jaw was in shooting pain. It was the holidays. I felt like it couldn't be worse...until I remembered the year before.

GNAAAAH!

When 4 PEOPLE dear to me threatened or attempted suicide. My first year sober the number of xmas suicide threats went to 0 and its stayed there since.

My first sober Xmas was great. Lots of old friends in town, happy times with family.

I started writing a graphic novel, something I'd never tried before.

Then it was New Years 2010. The morning that changed my life forever.

TOTAL GIBBERISH

Is he gonna die? Kill or hurt me? Get arrested? Get committed? How will we get home?

My boyfriend of 3 years & I got really high on K all night, then he flipped out, pulled me out of our cab & into traffic, screaming that we would crash. He screamed his head off & smashed his phone.

The next day I was over drugs. I was over parties. I knew mental illness was no joke. It could kill me.

"There is no magic booze substitute that is going to make life the awesome party I thought it used to be, except living each moment like it really is, and coming by a few moments of happiness honestly. Also, being stoned."

"I LOOK FORWARD TO THE NEXT DECADE OF COMING BY MY JOY IN MORE SUSTAINABLE WAYS."

2010 Tatiana was an all-new Tatiana!

Nobody STEPS to me, nobody puts HANDS on me, NOBODY raises their voice to me.

SHIT IS ON, FUCKERS!

Now - I've been yanked out of cars & thrown into traffic by men before! And how. But this was the first time I wasn't drunk for it. I felt it.

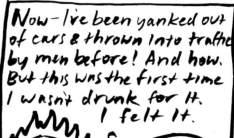

I found that to be... UNACCEPTABLE.

I had built a safe place. Now that I knew what it was like to feel safe, I wasn't about to give it up.

you come into my house there are rules.

My life got flipped turned upside down.

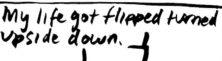

Drugs aren't awesome. They're dangerous. If not the drugs then the people who freak out on them. Being self destructive isn't cool. People can live their lives but I don't want to clean up the mess.

I figured out that no one had my back.

ME BEFORE

Where my friends are here thru thick & thin!

They help me!

ME AFTER

By the time the men in white coats come for you, everyone is gone.

No one is willing to put up with the mentally ill. No one.

Since I was going to be all alone no matter what, I stopped caring.

Oh you're worried my boyfriend is dangerous? Welcome to being blocked on Facebook, whore!

It didn't help that all my drunk "friends" were having a field day talking about it behind my back.

blah blah what a dumbfvck Tats is

I realized that's what happens when you only enjoy the company of malicious gossips- you reap what you sow.

I stopped telling people anything. They only use it against you.

You want to be FRIENDS, BITCH?!! I know what that means!

You want to fuck my boyfriend, talk shit behind my back, & feel superior to me! That's what FRIENDS do!!!!

SUPER

SOBRIETY GIRL

Behold as she abstains
from alcohol for a previously
unimaginable timespan of
1461 days-at-a-time!

SUPER
SOBRIETY
GIRL!

Powers of sensory
perception
✓ SEEING!
✓ HEARING!
✓ TASTING!
✓ SMELLING!
✓ CREATING!
✓ FEELING!
✓ THINKING!

Watch in awe
as she uses
COGNITIVE
PROCESS to
enhance her existence!

Celebrating six years without alcohol: January 2009-today

HOW TO QUIT DRINKING
(Tats' 12-steps, based on the AA 12-steps

Seek out alternative medicine & listen when they tell you how drinking is affecting your body

Have your doc tell you, only drink if you can 'give or take' it — not if you need it.

Realize since you're under the inflence for most social interaction, you don't have a clear picture of your life.

Realize the world is not a bad place & you are smart enough to excel, if you give yourself a chance.

Know as much as you hate not being in control, it's impossible. Make a list every morning of what you ARE in control of.

Breathing, behavior, diet, when you pee. Sometimes thats all, but it's enough.

Apologize without making excuses. Forgive yourself.

ITS OK

YOU'RE OK

Observe, don't judge, listen to yourself.

You do not have all the answers, admit it to yourself & the universe. You feel alone, unsure & afraid a lot.

Admit you've done bad things & hurt people, yourself included. We all have.

Be willing to take what comes, pay attention to the moment.

good things start to happen!

Ask the universe for help. Observe yourself & attempt to understand & forgive the way you are.

higher self

When anger is unbearable, chant: 'I love you, Thank you, I'm sorry, please forgive me.'

Contemplate all the damage you caused in running from your fears.

Write it down. There's going to be a lot

Start apologizing to those you feel bad about. Letters over email & in person.

sorry I was such a tool

Live in the now, directly communicate with those around you.

Remember you're not omnipotent. Apologize easily.

Relax, meditate, read books, stretch, excercise, & know you are exactly where you should be.

Hang out with one friend at a time. Sit under a tree. Watch a dog play.

Let everyone know! Talk with other sober people. Be open & honest. Help those who want to quit drinking.

Talk about it! Make new friends! Take risks!

sobriety

TATS

Made in the USA
San Bernardino, CA
15 May 2017